To my loving sister, BRYCE.
So sorry about the typo in the first book.
Thanks for understanding. You're the beast sister!
—AR

For Dave and Mike
—DS

Dial Books for Young Readers
Penguin Young Readers Group • An imprint of Penguin Random House LLC
375 Hudson Street • New York, NY 10014

Text copyright © 2017 by Adam Rubin
Illustrations copyright © 2017 by Daniel Salmieri

Library of Congress Cataloging-in-Publication Data
Names: Rubin, Adam, date, author. | Salmieri, Daniel, date, illustrator.
Title: Dragons love tacos 2: the sequel / by Adam Rubin ; illustrated by Daniel Salmieri.
Description: New York, NY : Dial Books for Young Readers, [2017]
Summary: "When dragons run out of tacos, they travel back in time to get a fresh supply"
—Provided by publisher.
Identifiers: LCCN 2016024850 | ISBN 9780525428886 (hardcover)
Subjects: | CYAC: Dragons—Fiction. | Tacos—Fiction. | Food habits—Fiction. | Humorous stories.
Classification: LCC PZ7.R83116 Drb 2017 | DDC [E]—dc23 LC record available at
https://lccn.loc.gov/2016024850

Printed in China • 11
Text set in Mikado • Designed by Jason Henry
The artwork for this book was created with watercolor,
gouache, color pencil, and digital.

DRAGONS LOVE TACOS 2

THE SEQUEL

ADAM RUBIN   DANIEL SALMIERI

Dial Books for Young Readers

Hey, kid!

Why are all your dragon friends crying?

They look so sad.

NO MORE TAC

WORLD IN SHOCK; EMERGENCY SUPPLIES DEPL

Taco Scientists Baffled

BY SEAN ARIANNEY

Top researchers admit they were blindsided by the sudden exhaustion of taco supplies. "We thought we had stocked up accordingly." Prof. Corey Von Mintz sighed. "Unfortunately, we grossly underestimated global demand." Newly calculated projections indicate that tacos may, in fact, be completely extinct. Recent studies suggest that

Congres
on

Lawmakers cal
in Washington M
crisis. Proposals
sides of the ais
be reached. Aft
ed debate, offic
tended recess. In
face mounting
and the lack of t
ing factor in the

Oh, my. We've got to do something about this.
LISTEN TO ME, DRAGONS: DON'T FREAK OUT!

No wonder they're upset: Dragons love tacos.

Remember that time we had an awesome taco party with dragons?

There were so many tacos. Pantloads of tacos.

Big tacos, little tacos, beef tacos, chicken tacos,

and because of a totally honest mistake (I'm not blaming anyone here) there were also some spicy tacos. Unfortunately, spicy salsa gives dragons the tummy troubles, and when dragons get the tummy troubles . . .

Well, you know.

But now, there are no more tacos. None. Nada. Nil.
If only we could somehow go back in time to our delicious
taco party (before the spicy salsa, of course). We could save a
handful of tacos, plant them in the ground, and grow taco trees
so we never run out of tacos again. The dragons would be so happy.

Well, I know we're not supposed to mess with it, but this does seem like the perfect opportunity to fire up that time machine in the garage.

A time machine lets you travel through time—
back to the past, when you were an itty-bitty
baby, or forward to the future, when you've
grown to be an old man!

Or in our case, back to the taco party full
of tacos.

You know what?

Let's strap into this gizmo and give it a whirl!

Set the dial to "taco party."

Ready, set . . .

Hey, that's you from before! Weird. Well, there are plenty of tacos here.
Let's just grab some and head back before the dragons eat any spicy—
Uh-oh.

Crunch,
crunch,
crunch.

Yikes. I sure hope this time machine still works.

Give the dial a little twist. We'll have to go a bit further back this time—*before* the dragons eat any spicy salsa.

Ready, set . . .

Hmmm. We may have gone a bit *too* far back. . . .

Crunch,
 crunch,
  crunch.

Oh boy, not again.

This time machine has seen better days.

Try some machine oil. That might do the trick.

Wait a second—
that's not machine oil!

This may complicate our journey through space-time.

Dragons love diapers?

That's not right. Let's try again.

Tacos love dragons?

Weird, but closer! One more time.

Dragons love tacos! That's it!

DRAGONS, QUICK: GRAB SOME TACOS AND LET'S
GET OUT OF HERE BEFORE IT'S TOO LATE!

Crunch,
    crunch,
        crunch.

Oh, come on.

You saved one. Phew!

We'll plant a tree and have tacos forever.
The dragons will be so happy.

After all, dragons love diapers.
I mean, tacos. Dragons love tacos.

Heck, everyone loves tacos.

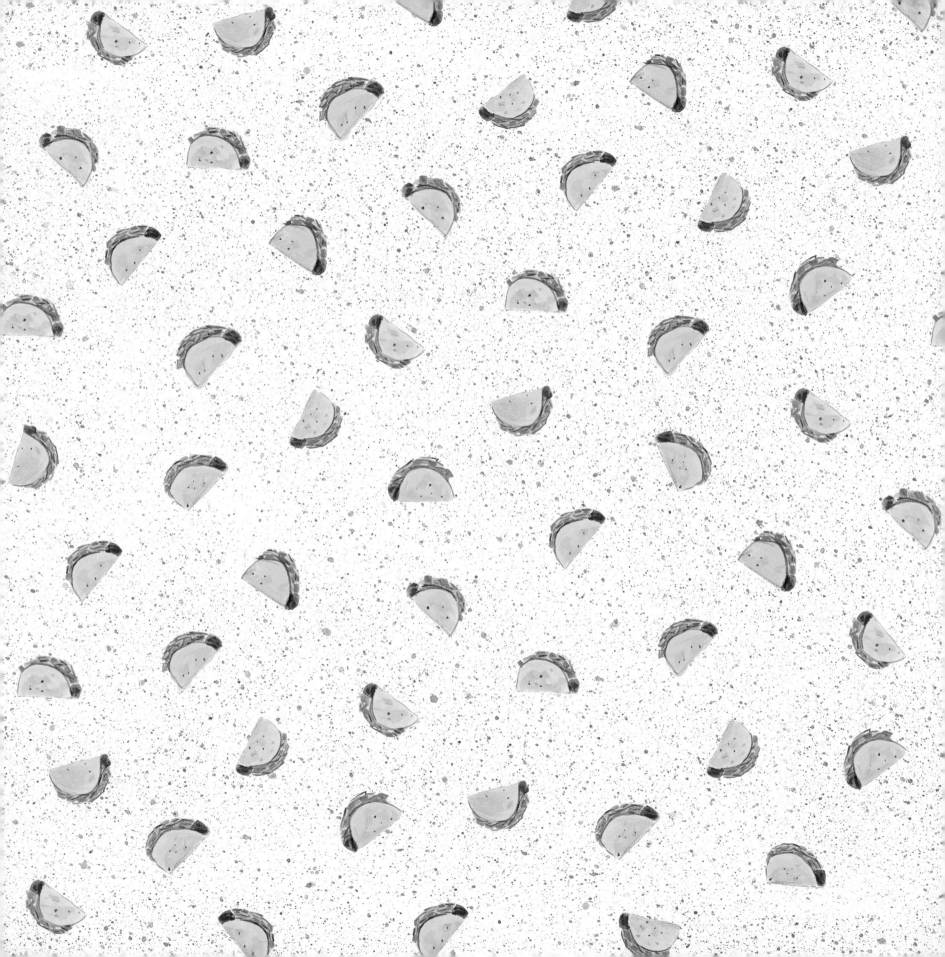